THE COLOR MONSTER

by Ron Fontes and Justine Korman
illustrated by Lynn Adams

GT
PUBLISHING
New York

Basil Brett, the world's greatest bunny detective, was spending a quiet Easter morning at home with his friend Dr. Hopson. Brett was about to eat his boiled egg when there was a loud knock on the door.

The Easter Bunny rushed into the room. "You've got to help me!" he cried. "Someone is stealing all the color off my Easter eggs!"

Brett put down his spoon and picked up his hat. "Come on, Hopson! The game's afoot!" he said.

Brett and Hopson followed the Easter Bunny to a sunny meadow.

"Here's where I hid the eggs. They used to be as bright as the crocuses — and now look at them!" the Easter Bunny wailed.

"Indeed," Brett muttered. The eggs were as white as his breakfast egg. Brett pointed to a trail of pale footprints crossing the meadow. "Look! It's as if whoever is stealing the color out of the eggs is also sucking it right up from the ground."

"Let's follow the white tracks to the color thief," suggested Dr. Hopson.

Brett agreed. "That's elementary, my dear Hopson."

So the detective team followed the pale trail. They followed it over hill and over dale, through forests and fields. The farther they followed it, the more nervous they got, and the more quietly and carefully they crept. Finally they tiptoed around a large rock — and almost ran into a huge monster! Even as they watched, the monster picked up a brightly-colored egg. It faded to white in his paws.

"Egad!" gasped Hopson. "The color monster!"

"Stop right there!" Brett cried. "You're under arrest for attempting to ruin Easter."

The monster looked surprised.

"I'm not trying to ruin Easter," he said. "I'm just trying to bring some of it home."

"Whatever do you mean?" asked Dr. Hopson.

"I come from the Land of Bland," the monster said. "Everything there is just plain white. Your world is so beautiful — especially these Easter eggs — that I wanted to bring home some color to share with my friends."

"How did you get here?" Brett asked.

"I found a brightly-colored door in the middle of the white woods," the monster explained. "When I opened it I found myself here in your colorful world. I really didn't mean any harm."

"That's all well and good. But we can't just leave these Easter eggs white, can we?" Dr. Hopson said.

"No, we can't. I'm afraid you'll have to re-color each one," Brett told the monster.

Soon the monster was hard at work repainting all the eggs.
"This is fun!" he cried. "I wish I could do this all the time."

"You can," Brett said. "In fact, I've got an idea."
After a quick trip to the art supply store, the monster was
ready to go home and start his new career.

The color monster became the first artist in the Land of Bland. Once the citizens saw what he could do, they voted to change the name of their country to the Site of Bright.

Back home, Brett tapped his spoon against a bright, freshly-cooked egg.

Dr. Hopson grinned. "You've cracked another case."

"Eggs-actly," replied the great detective.